Merv the Magpie

Mission 4JJ

Sharron Parle

Illustrated by Abbie Strain

Table of Contents

Dedication   02

Merv the Magpie   03

Epilogue   30

Old Tawny's Question Time   32

Acknowledgements   33

About the Author   34

Dedication

Merv the Magpie is dedicated to Thomas Kingdom Parle and the amazing children of 4JJ, Farnworth CE Primary School, Widnes.

Sharron Parle x

Merv the Magpie

In the North of England there is a town called Widnes, in that town there is a school called Farnworth and in that school, there is a classroom, it is empty. If you were ever to stand in that classroom and look out of the window you would see some trees where the children like to hide and play once the day has ended.

If you wandered ever so quietly amongst those trees and looked up into the leafy branches you might be surprised to see a nest, Merv's nest.

Merv would be extremely pleased to see you!

This is the nest where Merv hatched from his greeny-blue egg exactly one year ago. The rest of his brothers and sisters have flown away and found homes of their own, but Merv loves his nest with its view of the classroom so much so that he decided to stay.

Merv the Magpie

The classroom is empty, the school is almost empty, his favourite children are nowhere to be seen. Merv was worried, he knew that something was amiss, this was not quite like any other holiday for the school.

At first, he quite liked the peace and tranquillity as he strutted around the playground preening his feathers, he visited the frogs in the pond, he explored the abandoned playground and peeked through the windows of all of the classrooms looking with envy at all of the brightly colourful and shiny things that adorned the walls.

After a week or two Merv was no longer enjoying the stillness and quiet, he longed for the chaos and the laughter. He also had a feeling in the pit of his gizzard that he had never, ever felt before. Merv was lonely.

He really must find the children he decided, he stretched out his iridescent wings and pushed off from the branch. He circled the empty playground and with a tiny bit of hope in his heart he flew off to meet the Parliament.

A Parliament is a name for a group of Magpies, it isn't like a Human's Parliament although some of the older Magpies can be a bit pompous and do sometimes fall asleep in the middle of a meeting. He was sure that the other Magpies would know what to do. After much chattering and flapping of wings, it was decided that Merv could go forth and find his children. To do so he first must go to the place of knowledge where a curious Magpie can find out almost anything, Merv set off at once.

The streets below were silent and empty except for the man dressed in red who posted things through the slots in the front of the houses and the fat pigeons looking extremely pleased with themselves as they bumbled around on the ground. 'They might not be feeling so pleased or fat soon.' thought Merv sadly as he flew over the chip shop and the other take away places that were closed and abandoned by the Humans.

He arrived at the park to the sound of honking from the swans and geese around the lake. The ducks waddled and the Moorhen glided silently through the reeds. Absent were the families grasping bags of bread, no children played on the swings. The park was empty except for the birds. Amongst the thicket of trees alongside the lake a cacophony of bird song could be heard, he had reached The Internest.

The Internest is by far the best place to find out just about anything, birds come and go tweeting new information all the time. Not all the information is accurate but Old Tawny tries to keep order the best he can.

"Hi Tawny." cawed Merv. "I need some information about my missing children."

"Congratulations! I didn't know you had any. When did they hatch?" hooted Tawny.

"Not my actual children, my little humans from the school, they have disappeared, I really need to find them."

Old Tawny yawned, it was way, way past his bedtime. "The word on the tweet is that all the Humans are in hiding from some sort of dangerous virus. Possibly something to do with a bat, a Pangolin and a cooking pot, and before you ask I have no idea what a Pangolin is but I did hear that a boy called Thomas has been trying to figure out a cure." hooted Tawny. Another voice squawked "I heard it's a zombie apocalypse caused by telephones!"

"That's enough out of you Crazy Pete, you're on your last warning now get off my branch!"
"Potato!" squawked Crazy Pete as he adjusted his hat made from tin foil and departed. "Stay awhile and ask around, I'm sure you will find the information you need. Good luck and stay safe my Corvid friend, I'm off to bed." Merv hopped around the Internest for the remainder of the morning listening to the twitters and witters of the visiting birds, taking note of all the places he needed to visit. All in all, it had been a very productive day. After supper Merv said a little Magpie prayer for all his brave children safe at home with their families, he crossed his feathers, closed his eyes, and went to sleep wishing for a cure.

Merv the Magpie

Merv was pleasantly surprised to find out just how close some of the children lived, he could even see one home from his nest!

He hopped onto the windowsill and peered in through the glass, there at a table sat his lovely Isla. She was writing in neat lines. He imagined that she was writing a story for her little brother who lay watching cartoons. A small pink object on the step caught his eye, it was a button. 'I will keep this to remind me.' he thought and with that, he picked up the button and flew back to his nest.

He had heard at the Internest that Zane also goes by the name of Zany O and that he makes videos on the Human internet. Merv was not entirely sure what the videos could be about but true enough there he was sat by his computer. Merv sat a while watching Zane. 'One day this kid's going to be a TV star!' he thought. As he readied himself to take flight he saw a shiny card amongst the flowers. It had a picture of a strange creature on it and the word Pokémon, he had never heard of a Pokémon before but apparently, according to the card, you've gotta to catch em all! 'I'm sure he won't miss this.' mused Merv and with that thought he picked up the card in his beak and flew back to his nest.

Merv felt happier than he had done for days, he looked at the new additions to his nest. The pink button brightened the place up and the sun reflected off the Pokémon card. Suddenly he knew what he would do, he would visit all the children in turn and collect an object to remind him of his wonderfully crazy little Humans. In just one day he had collected the treasures from Isla and Zane, he had visited Ivan and was surprised to find that he had lots of siblings just like him. They all looked so happy that he decided that when he had finished his mission he must go and see his brothers and sisters and tell them all about his adventure. While he was hopping around in the garden he had found a beautiful swirly marble, it was particularly difficult to pick up with a beak but he'd managed in the end.

He found an eraser shaped like a football in Kylan's garden and a beautiful shiny pebble on Laila's doorstep. Kylan had been indoors with his brothers River and Baylen, he was playing Hello Neighbour but when Merv fluttered by, all three boys rushed to the window to salute him on his way. 'Such polite children!' thought Merv. He had found Laila crouched down beside a

bramble bush. It looked like she might be picking blackberries but Merv had known that she was looking for fairies. He hoped she wasn't planning on wrestling with them, they might be small but Merv knew that they can be very, very strong!
Feeling very satisfied with himself Merv settled down t
roost for the night.

After a nutritious breakfast of beetle bums and half a caterpillar, Merv was ready for the day's mission. First up was Thomas, his house was easy to find because of the four cherry blossom trees in the front garden. It was still exceedingly early but there he was running barefoot on the grass holding onto what looked like a yellow rubber chicken without feathers. 'This must be the fabled Chicken Wing Fred.' he thought as he sat a while amongst the pink blossoms. On the pavement next to a drawing of a rainbow was a piece of yellow chalk, he had seen Thomas at school in his yellow raincoat and knew yellow was his favourite colour, he thought that the chalk would be the perfect memento.

Next, he flew onwards to Neave's house where he found her in the garden practising her gymnastics while her baby brother William watched and tried to join in, there nestled in the new vegetable garden he found a little button in the shape of a ladybird, that will do nicely thought Merv.

Dexter was running around his garden as Merv flew overhead, he tried to keep up but Dexter was very, very fast and the Magpie had to stop in the tree while he waited for a dizzy spell to pass. When he woke from his snooze Dexter had gone but there on the path lay his trainers. Merv flew down and after much huffing and puffing managed to remove one of Dexter's laces.

With a button in his beak, a piece of yellow chalk in his left claw, and a lace in his right claw Merv made his way back to his nest and arranged his new treasures. This was much, much better and the strange feeling in his gizzard shrank a little as his beaky smile grew bigger.

The next morning he awoke bright and early, he polished off the rest of the caterpillar and once again set about his quest, as he flew it occurred to him that there was such a lot of work to be done before his collection was complete. He decided that he most definitely could do with some help.

His first call of the day was to see Ella and he was delighted when he saw not only Ella but her little sister Lily too. They painted and crafted in the sun while he looked on, Merv was not too sure what they were making but it was bright and shiny and therefore he very much approved. He waited until they went in for a snack before swooping down and helping himself to a small tub of glitter, he went on his way leaving a sparkling trail in the sky behind him as he flew.

He stashed the glitter in his nest and set off once again for Parliament, he was met with much interest as his wings glistened and sparkled in the sun.

"I really need some help." chattered Merv. "It's a much bigger job than I anticipated, some of these children do live quite a way out of the catchment area."

"And what, dare I ask is a catchment area?" asked one of his brethren on the branch.

"I have no idea." said Merv, "I heard it on the Internest, but the point is I do need some assistance."

As usual, before any decision was made there was much flapping and chat chattering. Finally, the Parliament agreed and Merv told the other Magpies about his plan. Merv chose 3 trustworthy fellow Magpies that he thought would make a good team. He gathered them together the very next morning

"Right then." he said "This is the plan, I will visit all of the children and then you, my friends, if you would be so kind, will go on a mission to collect the keepsakes for my nest. We will keep in touch via the Internest."

"Do we have a name for this plan?" croaked Bert.

"Mission 4JJ." replied Merv.

"What's a 4JJ?" asked Groovy.

"A 4JJ is.....mmm....its smiles, kindness, laughter, and togetherness all rolled up in a scrumptious bundle of small people." said Merv.

"I might need to get one of those for myself." cawed Alice wistfully.

"I highly recommend it!" Merv replied and with much flapping of black and white wings Mission 4JJ was underway.

Merv consulted his list of addresses and swooped down, he landed on the windowsill and peeked inside. There he spied the biggest dog he had ever seen in his life. That must be Digby he thought and sure enough, India was calling his name whilst laughing and ruffling the giant dog's fur. "I could sit here all day." he sighed "but I must get on."

Onwards he flew, he turned right at the corner shop and there it was, the road where Arianna lives. He flew to the top of the chimney and from up there he spotted them in the garden. The whole family was there Arianna, Aurelia, and Atticus singing away while their Daddy played the guitar, their Mummy watched with her fingers in her ears, but she wore the biggest smile.

He listened to the end of the song, stretched his wings and away he went.

Next, he circled some new houses while he got his bearings, in the olden days there used to be a big schoo here but now it was gone and in its place, there are houses full of happy families. In one of these houses, h knows he will find Nathan and his brother Jack. He lands on the fence post, warily eyeing the two black cats that were lazing in the sun, he did not have to wait long for the boys to come out wearing their swimming shorts. They climbed into a big bubbling poo and splashed each other, shrieking with laughter. One of the cats spotted him and so with a mighty flap of h wings he was gone.

There are two children in Class 4JJ called Sophia but th Internest had not been able to tell him which lived where so he flew to the next address not quite knowir who he would see. As he swooped down for a better view, there in the sunshine was Sophia F practising her dance moves to a groovy tune, she was incredibly good even her brother Thomas looked like he was impressed Merv was feeling so happy that he vowed to do a little dance of his own as soon as he got back to his nest.

Onwards, once more he heads off into the cloudless sk he hopes he will be able to see Sophia S. Even before h sees them, he hears Sophia and Luca laughing as they slip down the slide into their pool with an almighty splash.

By now the day was cooling and it was almost time to head back to roost for the evening, first though he must visit the Internest and pass on his information so that Alice, Bert, and Groovy could be successful in their treasure hunt.

Opposite the park not far from the Internest lives Harley and so Merv felt it was only polite that he should call on his way. He alighted on the hedgerow so that he could get a good view inside the house. There on the couch snuggled together under a blanket was Harley, Jenson, and Emmi. They munched popcorn and pizza, pointing and laughing at the cartoon on the TV. They all looked so very content. This was definitely helping to shrink the lonely feeling in Merv's gizzard.

Eventually, he reached the ancient gnarled tree just in time for Old Tawny to emerge from his sleep. "How are you getting on with your mission young Merv? I hear you have a team of helpers now."

It's all coming together nicely." said Merv "I'm feeling much, much better and I have seen almost half of the children already!"

Excellent news." hooted Tawny "Just download your information to the birds on the branch below and we'll make sure your team knows what to do."

Merv arrived back at his nest and was so tired that he whistled for a takeaway. While he waited, he thought about his day and realised that the horrible lonely feeling was getting much, much smaller, and was being replaced instead with a lovely warm feeling. Soon his caterpillar with extra flies arrived, he ate quickly and once he had finished he flew down to the classroom

doorway to celebrate the end of a satisfying day with a
little dance just like Sophia's

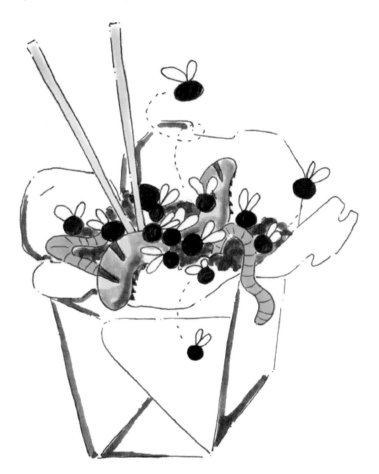

BERNARD'S BUG-TASTIC TAKEAWAYS

DELIVERED RIGHT TO YOUR NEST!

TODAYS SPECIAL

CATERPILLAR SURPRISE WITH EXTRA FLIES

The sun came up and the sky was once again blue and cloudless. It was going to be a good day.

The first call of the morning was to see Isobel, she was sat outside eating her breakfast. Playing at her feet was the smallest, cutest little puppy he had ever seen and not for the first time Merv thought about how nice it must be to have a little pet to come home to every day. The puppy's name was Reggie, Merv once had an Uncle Reggie but he was extremely grouchy and nowhere near as cute.

From Isobel's house, he had quite a journey, when he eventually saw the roundabout next to The Crow's Nest (which was not really a crow's nest at all!) he knew he had almost reached Oliver's house. Oliver was playing on his computer game with a look of concentration on his face, his sister Ava was dressed as a princess and lay on the floor beside him colouring in a book chatting to him as he played. Merv's next stop was Fionntán's, this was not so far and within a minute or two he was flying over the top of his house. He could hear someone playing a keyboard, he circled lower and lower until he could see Fionntán hitting the keys with gusto while his big sister Téagán read a book on the sofa. Twinkle and Coco yapped enthusiastically along to the tune and his Mummy was drinking her tea with a wistful look that suggested she could probably do with something much stronger.

From here Merv flew out over the fields until the town seemed quite far away. Eventually, he came to another Crow's Nest but this wasn't a nest either, it was a farm. This was William's farm where he lived with his Mummy, Daddy, and his little sister Grace in a big barn which was far too fancy for the farm animals to live in anymore. His grandparents lived here too in the big farmhouse. Today William and Grace were out in the tractor with Daddy, Merv joined the seagulls that followed the tractor as it churned up beetles and worms in its wake. He followed them once more around the field before taking to the sky again and heading back across the fields towards the town.

 As he made his way above the winding country lane, he saw an empty car park. He knew that this was the place where Humans went to buy plants and small colourful people to put in their gardens. He also knew that this must mean that he was almost at Tilly's house. As he came to land on the roof of the summer house, he thought he could smell owls, lots and lots of owls. 'How very strange' thought Merv.

Tilly was at the table with her Mummy, they looked remarkably busy, Tilly sorted buttons into pairs and her Mummy was sewing on a machine. They were making headbands, someone at the Internest had mentioned this. He'd heard that they were for helping Drs and nurses ears stay safe from the virus. Merv tore himself away from the very tempting sight of the buttons and with a flap of his wings took to the sky once again.

From Tilly's he flew over the expressway, he looked down at the empty road. Normally cars and lorries zoomed along there and on really busy days they snaked slowly along like a procession of multicoloured beetles, but today nothing zoomed or snaked.
He flew along where the houses met the fields, eventually, he came to a lane, he followed the lane down to the house where Alex lived. Alex has a sister, her name is Cara, Merv could see her sat in the sun, beside her was a little pile of daisies and she was delicately threading them together one by. As he got closer still, he spied Alex sat cross-legged watching wrestling on the TV inside. It was called WWE evidently. He wasn't sure what that meant but the boy seemed to be enjoying it anyway so that was plenty good enough for Merv.
He flew back along the lane towards his next destination but first, he stopped on an anthill for a snack and a rest, he preened his feathers and vowed to

21

come for an Anting sometime soon. Having an Anting is the bird equivalent of going to a Spa, you really must make the ants quite cross though and you most definitely do not get a cup of coffee!

Feeling refreshed he set off once again, he arrived just in time to see a very impressive dance display featuring Daisy and her little sister Bella. He could feel his feet tapping and he decided he was so incredibly lucky to have such talented children to visit.

He finished his day off with another trip to the Internest before heading back to roost for the night. As he was leaving the park, he spotted Faith jogging with her mummy, he decided to tag along for a while and flew overhead as they jogged and chatted. They did a whole lap of the park together before Merv set off for his nest again. As he approached, he could see a small pile of objects in the grass at the foot of his tree. Mission 4JJ was most definitely proving to be a success. Groovy, Bert, and Alice had brought him a hair bobble belonging to India, a triangle type thing that humans used to play the guitar from Arianna, a beautiful glass heart from Nathan's garden that surely must have needed two of them to carry, a hair clip from Sophia F, a yellow button from Sophia S and a small toy car from Harley. 'I think I'm going to need a bigger nest.' thought Merv as he admired his keepsakes and snuggled down for the night.

B right, early and breakfasted, Merv was ready to take on the day.
'I will pay Archie a visit next.' thought Merv
Archie was already wide awake
and surrounded by little
coloured bricks, it looked like
he was building a house or a
shop. It was very impressive
and Merv wondered if perhaps
Archie could build him an
extension for his nest. His little
sister Annabelle was trying to help sort the bricks, it
did not look like it was helping very much at all but as
Merv remembered Archie truly is a kind and patient
boy.
Merv took flight once again and set off to visit George.
He was sat reading in the garden, he had a book all
about animals and was reading facts aloud to his
younger brother William. 'I wonder if there's anything
about me in there?' pondered Merv.
'Did you know that the Latin name for a Magpie is Pica
Pica?" said George to his brother. "Can I have a biscuit
now?" replied William and skipped off into the house.
'Fame at last!' thought Merv to himself and away he
flew.
"Oh my, what a delicious smell." chirped a small
sparrow who was hopping about excitedly on Jessica's
step.
"It is indeed." agreed Merv "I expect it's my little friend
Jessica, she can bake a mean cake!" and true enough

there was Jessica in the kitchen with Mummy, they were both covered in flour, her big brother Samuel played on his computer game in the next room.

He vowed to come back later to see if he could find a crumb or two, he shot upwards making his way through the clear skies, the roads below still quiet and devoid of traffic. The air around him most definitely felt fresher and cleaner than usual and he wondered if it was because the Humans were at home instead of driving in their cars or jetting off on their holidays.

He could hear a familiar noise, it was the sound that is made when a leather boot meets a leather ball. Below him in the garden was Billy kicking his football, he had some very fancy footwork. A Magpie's claws are not made for kicking a ball but even if they were Merv doubted he would be as good as Billy.

'4JJ is a very sporty lot.' thought Merv as he cut through the air on his way to visit Zara.

Zara cartwheeled across the garden towards her sister Olivia. They practised handstands and backflips. They couldn't go to their gymnastic club but they were certainly getting plenty of practice in the sunshine.

Merv was feeling very, very tired but as he only had two more children to see he pushed on soaring high above the houses as he made his way to see Alicia and her little brother Elliot. He flew down and perched upon the windowsill and peeked inside. Alicia was painting a beautiful rainbow while her brother looked on.

Merv read the message on the picture, it was for her Nanny Elaine to put in her window. He had seen many,

many houses with rainbows in the windows over the days he had been flying on his mission. Thinking of all the wonderfully coloured keepsakes he would soon have to adorn his nest Merv took flight to visit the last of his children.

He looked down from the sky into the garden and there he was, last but most definitely not least, was Olivia. She balanced gracefully as she walked across a beam in her garden, she did not wobble at all even when her brother Evan's ball came bouncing towards her! This must be some more of that gymnastic thing he had been seeing a lot of recently, he thought.

He fluttered down into the branches of a tree and took a well-deserved rest amongst the leafy twigs. He thought about all the children that he had managed to catch a glimpse of and realised that finally he no longer felt lonely at all.

After his daily visit to the Internest was complete he set off for home. Once again as he approached his tree, he could see a small pile of goodies that lay waiting in the grass. A small biscuit in the shape of a bone, 'this must be from Isobel' thought Merv as he remembered tiny Reggie. A small bouncy ball from Oliver, a toy figure of a boy with a metal foot from Fionntán. Another Pokémon card, this time from William. He hopped about with excitement. "I am collecting Pokémon cards just like a human!" he exclaimed aloud. From Tilly, he had a scrap of bright material, a card with a WWE written on it, and a picture of a man with very big muscles from Alex. A daisy from Daisy and a ribbon from Faith. He transported them one by one up to his nest and set about arranging them artfully.

The next morning Merv awoke and could barely
contain his excitement, for today Alice, Bert and
Groovy would bring him the last batch of
mementos from the children and his collection would be
complete.

After a nutritious breakfast of earthworm with berries,
he busied himself tidying his nest and rearranging the
decor in preparation.

In the distance he could see 3 small black and white
shapes flapping, they quickly became bigger as they
flew swiftly towards his tree. It was Alice and the gang.
They must have started rather early that morning.
He swooped down to the ground to greet them and the
four of them together did a small Magpie jig of
happiness.

Alice had brought a red building brick from Archie, a
small toy lizard from George, and a pretty cupcake case
from Jessica. Groovy proudly showed off his trove, a
coin from Billy, and a pink pen from Zara. Lastly, Bert
produced a small bottle of nail varnish from Alicia and a
shiny sweet wrapper from Olivia.

4JJ Mission was completed!

"How can I ever thank you enough?" exclaimed Merv.

"It's been fun." said the three friends together.

"We've decided that when all the Humans come out of
their houses once more we're going to rebuild our nests
near to other classrooms so we can have a 4JJ too!" said
Bert

"There really is only one 4JJ, but you'll find your own
group of special little Humans too." said Merv

"Oh, I've also got a very important message for you from Old Tawny." cawed Alice. "It seems that there are some very, very brave Humans, Doctors, Nurses, Carers, Teachers and people doing all sorts of jobs in shops and factories who have been trying to make people better and to keep things working until the Virus has been defeated. Every Thursday at 8 pm the Humans come ou of their houses into the street and clap and cheer, some even bang pans and toot car horns, all to say thank you to the heroes!"
"That's amazing" gasped Merv feeling a little tearful. "We will spread the word and join them, every week to say thank you for keeping our little friends safe and sound!" And with that, the four friends had a feathery hug and vowed to meet again on Thursday at 8 pm and every Thursday thereafter.
The towns are still empty, the streets are still empty,the classroom is still empty, but it won't be forever. The people will come out of their houses soon, the roads and schools will be busy once more and when they are the Magpies will be waiting. So, for now, remember, if by chance you are playing in your garden, on a walk with your family or stood on your doorstep at 8 pm on a Thursday and you happen to see a Magpie, give him a big wave. It is most probably Merv and if you are lucky enough to see more than one Magpie it could be Alice, Bert, and Groovy too!

Epilogue

It is June 2020 and the Humans are slowly starting to emerge from their homes, like butterflies emerging from their chrysalises, slowly drying their wings in the sun, summoning the courage to fly off into the blue skies and their new world.

Children are returning to the parks and schools, and grown-ups are returning to work. The streets and roads are a little busier and shops begin to open.

Heaven has gained lots of new angels and they, like Merv and his friends, continue to look down upon the children of the world and hope for gold at the end of all the rainbows.

The End

"A 4JJ is.....mmm....its smiles, kindness, laughter, and togetherness all rolled up in a scrumptious bundle of small people." said Merv.

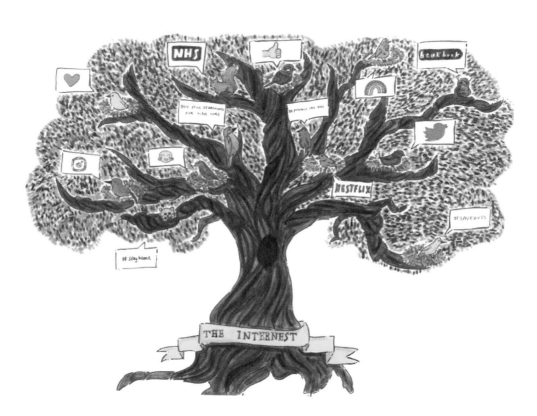

Old Tawny's Question Time

- How many pets did you count in the story?
- What musical instruments are played?
- A group of Magpies is a Parliament, what other group of birds has the same name?
- Merv sees lots of rainbows on his travels, how many of 4JJs rainbows does he see?
- Can you name all the other animals mentioned in the story?
- Describe a Pangolin.
- Name all of the human characters in the story
- What type of bird do you think Crazy Pete is?
- Why do birds need to annoy ants when they are having an Anting?
- Can you name all of the treasures Merv collected during his mission?

Acknowledgements

Many thanks to the parents of the real children of 4JJ for allowing me to borrow them awhile for Merv's tale.

To Abbie, thank you for your beautiful illustrations and for giving up so much of your time to help bring Merv's story to life.

WhatsApp mums, thank you for being there and for helping to keep each other sane, and to Widnes Martial Arts and our Kuk Sool family thank you so very much for your support and for providing the routine and stability that's has kept us going while the days and weeks threatened to merge into one.

A huge thank you to all the teachers and staff at Farnworth CE School for always helping our children to be the very, best they can be.

To Mr. J and Miss J, it was a short time but the very, best of times – thank you on behalf of the children of 4JJ.

And lastly to Rob and Thomas (& the ferrets) I cannot imagine being locked down with anyone better!

There's a lot of thanks here and when this is all over it's going to be a hugfest, with gin, lots and lots of gin!

Sharron x

About the Author

Sharron Parle lives in Widnes in the North of England with husband Rob and their 9-year-old son Thomas Kingdom Parle. They share their home with Chicken Wing Fred (a rubber chicken without feathers) and two mischievous ferrets named Daisy and Wendal.

They love nothing better than getting their "Owl on" for the annual JustSo Festival with illustrator Abbie and her family.

Abbie is a Year 11 pupil and a kick-ass ninja!